Khadeejah Ahmed

This is Apple Tree Farm.

Mr. and Mrs. Boot live here with their two children, Poppy and Sam. They have a dog called Rusty and a cat called Whiskers. Ted drives the tractor and helps look after all the animals on the farm.

Mrs. Boot

Mr. Boot

Ted

Poppy

Sam

Rusty
the dog

Whiskers
the cat

Woolly
the sheep

Curly
the piglet

There are lots of animals
on Apple Tree Farm.

cow

calf

dog

pig

piglet

sheep

lamb

horse

donkey

bird

goat

duck

luckling

goose

cat

mouse

5

house

chimney

balloon

bicycle

car

roof

door

This is Poppy and Sam's house.

window

fence

gate

cloud

tent

stream

boat

fish

frog

path

bridge   **haystack**   **scarecrow**   **pond**

rabbit

Poppy and Sam play by the stream.

Outside the house

Mrs. Boot is washing the car.

Poppy is riding her bicycle.

The balloon is near a cloud.

car

bicycle

balloon

cloud

By the stream

Sam plays with his boat.

Poppy is trying to catch a fish.

A frog is hiding under the bridge.

A fish jumps out of the stream.

stream   boat   fish   frog   bridge

sandals

hat

panties

T-shirt

socks

dress

Mrs. Boot hangs
the laundry up.

shoes   sweatshirt   nightgown   shorts

jeans

shirt

ladder

caterpillar

tree

fox

apple

leaf

Poppy helps Mrs. Boot pick the apples.

bee

butterfly

swing

flower

beetle

snail

15

Hanging the laundry up

Rusty wants to play with a sock.

The cat is playing with the hat.

Sam's jeans are on the line.

Poppy is holding up her clean dress.

sock

dress

jeans

hat

16

Picking apples

Mrs. Boot
is standing
on a ladder.

Sam is sitting
on the swing.

Will Poppy
catch the apple?

A fox is hiding
behind a tree.

ladder   swing   fox   tree   apple

hen house

basket

worm

shovel

egg

Sam feeds the hens.

wheelbarrow

feather

18

bucket

hen

chick

bowl

mouse

straw

19

steam engine

track

signal

sandwich

bottle

juice

fork

cup

cheese

33

At the market

Mrs. Boot has a bunch of grapes.

Sam has potatoes and lettuce in his wheelbarrow.

How many cabbages is Poppy holding?

Will the pig eat the tomato?

 grapes  cabbages  potatoes  lettuce  tomatoes

34

Having a picnic

Poppy has dropped the bottle.

Mrs. Boot has a plate with cheese and a knife.

Sam is pouring the milk.

 bottle

cheese

 knife

 plate

 milk

computer

telephone

newspaper

photograph

video

picture

Poppy reads a book and Sam uses the computer.

radio   pencil   television   table

CD

pen

camera

chair

CD player

slippers

pillow

bed

teddy
bear

book

soap

brush

blinds

comb

mirror

sink

It is bedtime for
Poppy and Sam.

doll

toothbrush

toilet

39

At home

Poppy is
reading a book.

The telephone
is on the table.

Sam is using
the computer.

Mr. Boot is reading
a newspaper.

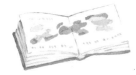   

book   telephone   newspaper   table   computer

Bedtime

Poppy's teddy bear is on the pillow.

Sam jumps on his bed.

The soap is on the sink.

Poppy brushes her teeth with her toothbrush.

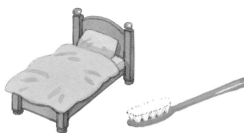    

bed toothbrush teddy bear pillow soap sink

Weather

snow

sun

rain

fog

wind

Seasons

spring

summer

rainbow

lightning

ice

cloudy

fall

winter

Colors

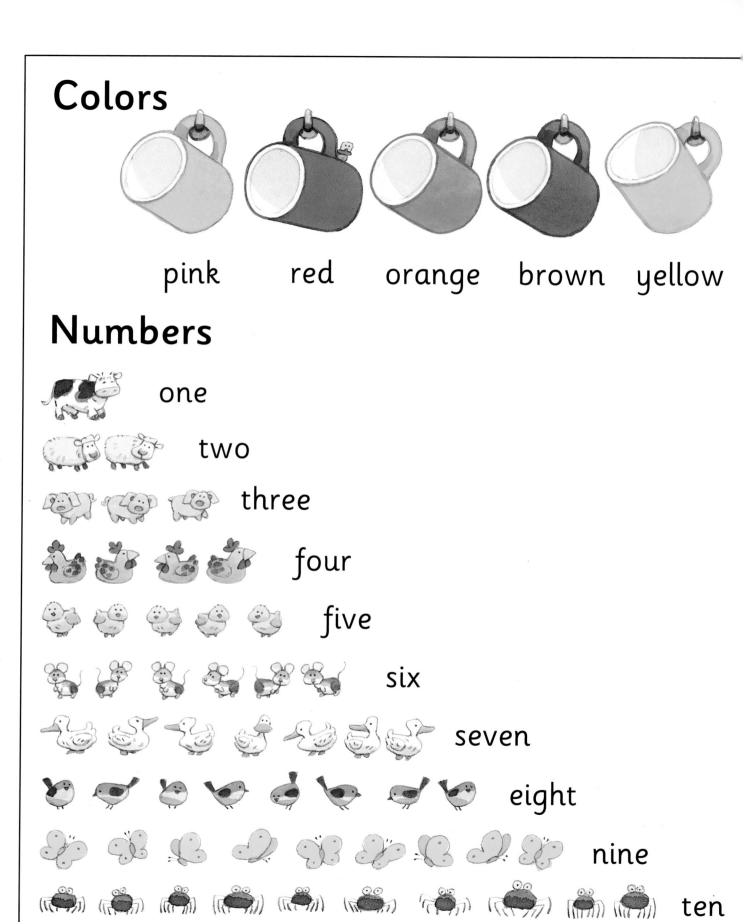

pink   red   orange   brown   yellow

Numbers

one

two

three

four

five

six

seven

eight

nine

ten

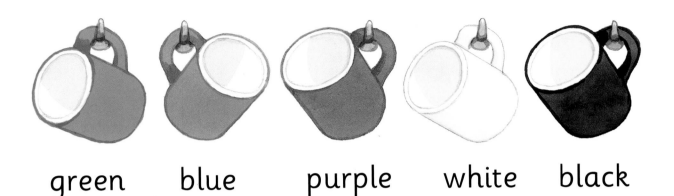

green   blue   purple   white   black

This is what **100** dogs look like.
Try counting them.

10
20
30
40
50
60
70
80
90
100

Word List

apple	cabbage	crab	frog
arm floaties	cake	cucumber	gate
bag	calf	cup	goat
ball	camera	Curly	goose
balloon	cap	dog	grapes
banana	car	doll	green
basket	carriage	donkey	hair
beans	carrot	door	hammer
bed	cat	dress	hand
bee	caterpillar	duck	hat
beetle	cauliflower	duckling	haystack
bicycle	CD	egg	head
bird	CD player	eight	hen
black	chair	engine	hen house
blanket	cheese	engineer	horse
blinds	cherries	fall	house
blue	chick	feather	ice
boat	chimney	feet	ice-cream cone
book	chocolate	fence	jeans
bottle	clock	fish	juice
bowl	cloud	five	knife
bread	cloudy	flag	ladder
bridge	coal	flower	lamb
brown	comb	fog	lamp
brush	computer	fork	leaf
bucket	conductor	four	lettuce
butterfly	cow	fox	lightning

milk	pond	signal	toilet
mirror	Poppy	sink	tomatoes
mouse	potatoes	six	tool box
Mr. Boot	purple	slippers	toothbrush
Mrs. Boot	rabbit	snail	towel
mushrooms	radio	snow	track
newspaper	rain	soap	tractor
nightgown	rainbow	sock	trailer
nine	red	spring	tree
one	roof	steam engine	T-shirt
onions	rope	steering wheel	two
orange	Rusty	straw	umbrella
paint	sack	strawberries	video
panties	Sam	stream	wheelbarrow
path	sandals	summer	Whiskers
pear	sandcastle	sun	white
peas	sandwich	sunglasses	wind
pen	scarecrow	sweatshirt	window
pencil	screwdriver	swing	winter
photograph	seat	table	Woolly
picture	seven	Ted	worm
pig	sheep	teddy bear	wrench
piglet	shell	telephone	yellow
pillow	shirt	television	yogurt
pink	shoes	ten	
plate	shorts	tent	
plums	shovel	three	

Can you find a word to match each picture?